DAFT DAVY

DAFT DAVY

A Story in Verse

Raymond Wilson

*To James
with every good wish*

Raymond Wilson

faber and faber

LONDON · BOSTON

First published in 1987
by Faber and Faber Limited
3 Queen Square London WC1N 3AU

Typeset by Goodfellow & Egan, Cambridge
Printed in Great Britain by
Redwood Burn Ltd, Trowbridge, Wiltshire
All rights reserved

British Library Cataloguing in Publication Data

Wilson, Raymond, *1925–*
Daft davy.
I. Title
821'.914   PR6073.I4/
ISBN 0-571-14548-5

Contents

Daft Davy
is born

There were thirteen chimes that midnight –
   One extra for hard luck –
And the tom-cat howled in the back street
   Like a creature struck.

The sky was a coal-black drizzle
   With never a star,
And the Tyne, the Tyne, the coaly Tyne
   Crawled on the dark like tar.

And there in the back-street bedroom,
   Under the weeping night,
Davy was born in a shuddering cell
   Of cold candlelight.

Davy, he wailed to the midwife's smack;
   The tom-cat howled outside,
Then crept in the backyard dustbin and
   Lay down and died.

There were thirteen chimes that midnight –
   One extra, as befits
A lad sold short, with only four
   Of his five wits.

he grows

He'd no Dad
And was glad,
Saw no call
For Mam at all;
But lived with Mad Blanche his sister, who
Nursed God's creatures in her backyard zoo:

A maimed cat,
A lame rat,
A bald mole
And sick vole,
The humble and halt, the broken and blind
Were the only family he'd ever find.

No one knew
How he grew;
No one cared
How he fared . . .
But grow he did, in a Tyneside slum,
Ginger and rough as a marmalade tom.

he didn't have a nurse

He didn't have a nurse by the name of Alice
With an interest in the Guards and Buckingham
    Palace;
But he had Mad Blanche, who would often give her
Cat and Daft Davy long walks by the river-
                     side.

He didn't have a house with spacious grounds
And good clean fun with the horses and hounds;
But he clung to the tailboard of a lorry
And rode triumphant – though secretly horri-
                    fied!

he is happy – and sad

When Davy was happy
Church bells were rung,
The pit-wheels twinkled,
The Swing Bridge swung,
The cats turned somersaults,
The dogs broke into song
And the ships at their moorings
Hooted all day long.

But when Davy was sad
The school bells were rung,
The cats yawned wide then
Swallowed their tongue,
The fog-horns groaned
And a dead dog swung
On a tide as black
As a pitman's lung.

he sees the countryside for the first time

'O coaly Tyne, *where* do you come from?' he cried,
As he pondered the river, down by Quayside;
But the question went drifting away on the tide.

Mad Blanche cut him sandwiches (onion and butter,
Tied in brown paper) and he walked in the gutter
That followed the river, too happy to utter

The feeling that set his glazed eyes in a dream,
For he wasn't as simple as he might seem:
It was Daft Davy Livingstone that moved upstream!

Past buffalo bollards crouched ready to charge,
And a huge floating hippo disguised as a barge
Where cranes, like stiff-necked giraffes, roamed
    at large;

And just there, where the railway lines curved on
    a bend,
And the great arc of river swept past the town's end
Into pasture and woodland, he had to defend

His eyes from the glare and the glory of green
With the blue sky above it, too bright to be seen,
And the coaly Tyne running both silver and clean!

he goes (sometimes) to school

Davy
was no fan
of the School Attendance man

Maybe
canes and schools
aren't really suitable for fools

the Law
still demanded
that school should be attended

what's more
the Headmaster
proclaimed him a disaster

being no
great bookworm
his liking for lessons was lukewarm

even so
he was fluent
in the art of playing truant

Davy's Christmas and New Year

The candled trees burned night and day,
and bicycles and roller-skates,
train sets, mouth organs, footballs lay
    in hummocks at their feet.

Toyless at Christmas, Davy spread
his face like flattened putty on
shop windows, glowing through the dead
    of night in Grainger Street.

Blinded as by kaleidoscopes
of tinsel, stardust, flashing lights,
how could he know his brightest hopes
    must darken to defeat?

. . . . . .

Outside St. Nicholas', New Year's Eve,
The throng, more dense than you'd conceive,
Link arms and dance, and hurl and heave
    In fond embraces,
With not so much as 'by your leave',
    And laughing faces.

With yammering teeth, goose-flesh a-quiver,
Davy lies huddled by the icy river,
The very soul of him a-shiver,
    When with a start
He hears the clamour, and wild bells give a
    Glow to his heart.

he reads to his teacher

'This . . . is . . . a boy. This . . . is . . . a cat . . .'
Davy's voice stumbles, and falls flat.
Teacher and boy together look
Intently at the hated book.

Knowing too well what that vague eye
And the slack, working mouth imply,
She wonders by what God-cursed chance
She's asked to make a cripple dance.

She doesn't and will never know
What makes his vague eyes wander so
From words to the drawing of a cat,
And shouts, as he strokes it, *'Don't do that!'*

they make fun of him

Barefoot in the back street
And cobbled lane,
For Davy the roaring boy
It was Abel and Cain
All over again.

'Ginger,' they yelled. '*Daft* Ginger!'
And his poor head dazed.
With eyes crossed and lolling tongue
They taunted him till, half-crazed,
His vague eyes blazed.

'Ginger, you're barmy!' screamed
The girls, and ran;
And loud-mouthed lads kept prodding:
'Show us you're a man
And fight if you can!'

Fight he did, like an alley-cat,
Both tooth and claw;
Down hooligan back lanes
He tussled and tore,
For ever at war.

Meanwhile his betters were busy
Blazing the trail
Of a war they called Great
(Respecting the scale
Of Somme and Passchendaele).

he grows from boyhood to manhood during the Depression

The games came round in their season –
  Hoops, tops and whips –
And disappeared for no reason;
  But both in and out of season
The loud-mouthed gangs went roaring day and night
Through street and playground, spoiling for a fight.

Borne on the dark tide of Time –
  Child, youth and man –
He came into his shabby prime,
  And white hairs flecked the ginger in time
As he busked, cap in hand, outside pub doors,
Or stood guard by the rag-and-boneman's horse.

And the twelve months slowly changing –
  Greens, browns and greys –
Were God's way of rearranging
  A world where nothing was changing
For the layabout lads who were waiting for
Jobs in munitions in the Second World War.

they take away his sister

When the full moon hung like yellow fruit
   On the boughs of a winter's night,
They put Mad Blanche in a hospital ward
   Because, they said, she'd no right
To sit and sing to her marmalade tom
   All in the cold moonlight.

'We've got to put her away,' they said,
   'For fear she does herself harm.'
But when Davy came at visiting time
   With the tom tucked under one arm:
'Get that beast out of here, and take yourself
   With it!' they cried in alarm.

When the next full moon like a Chinese lantern
   Hung in dark rafters of night,
They brought Blanche home in an ambulance . . .
   Even they couldn't bear the sight
Of her breaking her heart for her marmalade tom,
   All huddled in cold moonlight.

An Operetta
in which
he is condemned by
The Welfare State Choral Society

(The curtains rise to outraged cries)

The Inspector of Taxes, scowling:
>'Arrested for busking once more –
>And not one Tax Return to declare what you earn,
>After years of breaking the Law!'

The Welfare State Choral Society:
>*'He'll be kept off the street*
>*By police on their beat*
>*For such scandalous impropriety!'*

The Employment Officer, frowning:
>'You're a hangdog, indolent Nerk:
>Forty years on the dole, because – bless my soul! –
>You say you've no talent for work!'

The Welfare State Choral Society:
>*'We shall see that he cleans*
>*The workers' latrines*
>*As a punishment for impropriety!'*

The Housing Officer, sternly:
>'This Black Hole of Calcutta
>Is alive with more vermin than I can determine
>And no more like Home than a gutter!'

The Welfare State Choral Society:
> 'When we replan the town
> We will knock his house down
> To ensure there's no more impropriety!'

The Medical Officer, gravely:
> 'You stink like a kipper, my man,
> And as for your clothes, you've got more fleas
> in those
> Than a tinker's caravan!'

The Welfare State Choral Society:
> 'He must be disinfected
> And fully inspected
> And forbidden all such impropriety!'

(As the curtains descend, all voices blend.)

The Grand Chorus of the Welfare Society:
> We never forgive Contrariety!

> And therefore we must ask that you
> Will always without question do
> Precisely what we tell you to
> And take good care that you eschew
> The slightest impropriety!

he resists eviction, and triumphs
over the Lord Mayor

O Daft Davy and his sister Blanche,
    They lived by the riverside:
They fed on fish from a broken dish
    And dipped their bread in the tide.
They lit their fire with driftwood,
They washed in an old tin can;
For Blanche, she was hardly a lady,
And Davy was scarcely a man.

. . . .

The Lord Mayor, he came to see them,
    He came in a smart Rolls Royce.
'Daft Davy, I fear that you cannot live here,'
    He said in a Sunday-best voice.
'You must not light fires with driftwood,
Nor wash in an old tin can;
But Blanche, she must live like a lady,
And you like a gentleman.

'This riverside shack isn't fit for a cat,'
    Said the Mayor, and he held his nose.
'You must move out this minute – you must not live
    in it,
    So pack up your toothbrush and clothes.'
But Mad Blanche and her brother, Daft Davy,
Loved the shack in which they were bred:
'You can't turn us out, sir; we haven't a clout, sir,
And scarcely a tooth in our head!'

The Lord Mayor, he puffed with importance;
   He fingered his solid gold chain:
'I will give you a flat, with some chairs and a mat,
   And a roof that keeps out the rain.'
'Grant us time to collect our belongings,'
Said Blanche, with a dignified air;
'I've a marmalade cat, a piebald rat,
And some worms that I curl in my hair.'

'Will you kindly oblige and hold these, sir?'
   Davy said, and he spoke like a king:
'Two spiders, a vole, a toad and a mole,
   And cockroaches tied up with string.
There's an old violin to keep mice in,
A blanket for wrapping up snakes,
A bucket for beetles, a bowl for the nettles,
And flies for the currants in cakes.'

The Mayor he turned pink, then a pillar-box red,
   And at last a most delicate green.
'Pray hold open the door – we'll come back for more,'
   Said Blanche, and she spoke like a queen.
'Now since you insist we remove, sir,'
Davy said, as he nudged him aside,
'With things as they are, we'll just borrow your car
And take our pets for a ride.'

But the Mayor loved his Rolls with a passion,
   (Its leopard-skin seats were quite new)
And the mere thought of snakes coiled round his
   brakes
   Turned him a violent blue.
He leapt out of his car like elastic
When it's stretched and then cut with a knife:

'Keep your rat and your cat, keep your vole and your
     mole,
Keep your house and your mouse, keep your cakes and
     your snakes,
Keep your distance, I say, and don't dare move away,
Or I'll put you in prison for life!'

. . . .

So Daft Davy and his sister, Blanche,
     Lived on by the riverside:
They fed on fish from a broken dish
     And dipped their bread in the tide.
They lit their fire with driftwood,
They washed in an old tin can;
For Blanche was still far from a lady,
And Daft Davy was *no* gentleman.

Daft Davy at the seaside

(i)

The new day
Flooded the green bay
In a slow explosion of blue
Sky and silver sand and shimmering sea.
Boots in hand, he paddled the brilliancy
Of rippled wavelets that withdrew,
Sucking his splay grey
Feet in play.

(ii)

It was magic – the brightness of air,
the green bay and wide arc of the sea,
with the rock-pools reflecting his stare
and a maze of wind-sculpted sand-dunes where
slum streets and the Quayside should be.

It was music – not only the sound
of the buskers outside the pub door
and the band on the pier, but the pound-
ing of waves, the loud kids all around,
and gulls screaming shrill on the shore.

It was magic and music and motion –
there were yachts sweeping smooth in the bay
and black steamers white-plumed in mid-ocean;
and ice-cream, candy floss and commotion
as the Switchback got under way.

He clung
to the metal bar, clench-
ing it
TIGHT
as it swung
and wrench-
ed him
left, right
backforwards
sideways and Oh
up up up UP
(will it never touch the top?)
to a sick-
en-
ing
P
   L
      U
         N
           G
              E
and an end-
less
drop
drop
dropping
down
a dark pit-
shaft
that's Daft
Davy's stomach.
Then a sudden
lunge

and everything slows, steadies, slides
                                and glides
                            to a
                                STOP.

                        (iv)

            They let him stroke
            the donkeys. They
            told him he could,
            if he wished, stay
            and see them fed
            before the day
            ended. Their coats
            were shaggy grey.

            He liked their ears
            best, and the way
            they curled like sea-
            shells from the bay.
            He stood and watched
            them eat the hay,
            then patted them
            and went away.

                        (v)

              The spent day
           Drained from beach and bay
        Green and silver and shimmering blue.
        On prom and pier, arcade and B and B
    The looped lights dimly glowed. And he could see
        Stars winking at him, glimmering through
            The sky's moth-eaten grey
                As if in play.

                       [19]

he visits a farm

He walked in the country one Sunday,
    Dazed with the glare of green,
Then knocked and complained at the farmhouse:
    'There's never a beast to be seen!'

'Come,' grinned the Farmer, 'I'll show you!'
    And Davy was led
To where on the dark a herd of shadows
    Breathed in a sunless shed.

'Movement would toughen their meat,' he was told,
    'And daylight darken its hue.'
'Thank God,' cried Davy, 'I've only four wits,
    'If five make a man like you!'

'See here,' laughed the Farmer, and took him
    To a shed three times the size
Where row upon row of dim battery hens
    Pecked at their neighbours' eyes.

'To be fed, watered and warmed,' he said;
    'Who'd ask a kinder Fate?' –
But his voice came drowned in Davy's prayer:
    'Christ save them from the Welfare State!'

he is tested by the Psychiatrist

'Lie down on the couch, Daft Davy,'
   the Psychiatrist said,
'and tell me whatever happens to
   come into your head.'

So Davy lay still as a boulder
   and scowled at his toes,
and his thoughts were like the slow green moss
   that on a boulder grows . . .

'Just relax, and tell me your thoughts
   when you're no longer thinking . . . '
But the only sign of intelligent life
   was Davy's blinking!

'When I give you a word, make an effort
   to let your reply
come straight from an empty mind.' – Davy nodded,
   having no need to try!

The Psychiatrist paused and said, '*School*,'
   and Davy, 'A trampled bird's nest,
with God the Headmaster taking prayers
   and giving six of the best.'

'You must give only serious answers!'
   warned the Psychiatrist,
but his nervous tic got worse with each
   new word he took from his list.

'What of *Night*? – 'A crow.' – 'And *Day*?' – 'A swan.'
  'The *Sun*?' – 'A tinsel hawk.'
'The *Moon*?' – 'An owl with a hooded eye.'
  '*Stars*?' – Geese that fly and squawk.'

'Now tell me what *Welfare* means to you;
  just what does it recall?' –
'A Football Final where they play
  with a tom-cat for a ball!'

'Say what you see when you shut your eyes
  and everything's dark.' –
'Shadows chained from the fields and sun,'
  was Davy's remark.

'And what of your dreams, Daft Davy,
  what do you dream of in bed?' –
'I dream that I'm a chopping axe
  to chop down the Farmer's shed!'

The Psychiatrist twitched like a dowser's rod
  and begged him, 'Relax once more.' –
But Davy had fallen asleep on the couch
  and replied with a snore.

Daft Davy joins a CND march

They said the sky would catch on fire;
    They said the wind's hot breath
Would burn the shop, the pub, the street
And everyone you'd ever meet.
    They said it would be Death.

They said the world's best brains were racked
    Inventing a device
To kill all life and to ensure
That it stays dead for evermore,
    All for a Nobel Prize.

They said there'd be no dog, mole, mouse,
    And never a marmalade tom!
He marched with them along the Quay,
He sang he'd not be moved, and he
    Kept roaring, 'BAN THE BOMB!'

he walks, mumbling to himself

What was it he muttered, Daft Davy,
ignoring the throng
of fair, market, football-ground,
mouthing and mumbling and wailing,
with the shreds of his overcoat trailing
his patched boots as he shuffled along?

He made no more sense than the sound
of autumn wind in the leaves
or the gurgling of rain in a gutter
or the brawling of birds in the eaves,
and he'd stammer and spatter and splutter
like a quarrel of wind and rain
debating their age-old argument
time and again.

All nonsense! And yet, there were those who said
he'd some kind of second sight –
some lost instinct, by which he was led –
and, as a cat can see in the night,
so he could see in broad daylight
to walk and talk with the Dead!

. . . .

'And do you walk with the Dead, Davy?
    And do you talk with the Dead?' –
'And if I do, they're more real than you,'
    was all Davy said.

he is visited by a Professor
of Psychical Research

'They tell me,'
Said the Learnèd Authority,

'That you are
In touch with psychic phenomena.'

Davy's jaw
Fell open almost to the floor.

'Would you mind
Explaining precisely just what kind

Of a creature
You see, down to the very last feature?'

'All I see's . . .
Nothing,' said Davy, 'in two's and three's.'

'Ah, then they
Must have some vital message to convey?'

Davy said,
'The vital message is they're dead!'

he is evicted

Dear Sir or Madam,
This letter's to say
Your property
Stands bang in the way
Of Progress, and
Will be knocked down
On March the third
At half past one.

There is no appeal,
Since the National Need
Depends on more
And still more Speed,
And this, in turn,
Dear Sir or Madam,
Depends on half England
Being tar-macadam.
(But your house will –
We are pleased to say –
Be the fastest lane
Of the Motorway.)

Meanwhile the Borough
Corporation
Offer you new
Accommodation
Three miles away
On the thirteenth floor
(Flat Number Q
6 8 2 4).

But please take note,
The Council regret:
No dog, cat, bird
Or other pet;
No noise permitted,
No singing in the bath
(For permits to drink
Or smoke or laugh
Apply on Form
Z 3 2 7);
No children admitted
Aged under eleven;
No hawkers, tramps
Or roof-top lunchers;
No opening doors
To Bible-punchers.

Failure to pay
Your rent, when due,
Will lead to our
Evicting you.

The Council demands
That you consent
To the terms above
When you pay your rent.

Meanwhile we hope
You will feel free
To consult us
Should there prove to be
The slightest case
Of difficulty.

With kind regards,
Yours faithfully . . .

he sings a Song of Progress

No one can hold back Progress,
   It's going like a bomb;
But after the explosion
   There'll be no more marmalade tom.

The sports cars blur down motorways
   On endless journeys from
Nowhere hell-leather to nowhere,
   For Progress must go on.

And Progress has an army
   And weapons at command –
The brown-armed Irish navvies
   Are marching through the land!

The highway's patched with pancakes
   Where hedgehogs made their stand,
But farm and house and bird's nest
   Are pancakes Progress planned.

A timber shack and backyard zoo
   Aren't worth a string of beans –
Bulldozers have no tears to weep,
   Nor rich men's limousines.

O, it's too, too late for braking,
   Though you peer through dark windscreens
At the pile-up of all Progress
   And a world in smithereens!

he is brought on a charge before
the Magistrate

'Charged with obstruction, sir,' the Sergeant said.
Daft Davy stood erect and scratched his head.

'Please ask the witnesses to rise and state
Their testimony,' said the Magistrate.

'Threatened us with his mangy dog, your Honour,'
Said navvies Burke, Fitzpatrick and O'Connor.

(The Sergeant, sharp as mustard, added, 'Sir,
He's got no licence for the wretched cur.')

A spokesman said, 'He won't, at any price,
Do what he's told by Citizens' Advice.'

'Refused to quit his house, though in my letter,'
The Town Clerk said, 'I offered him one better.'

'If he's not forced to move, he'll throw a spanner
Slap in the Works of Progress,' said the Town
  Planner.

'Hum . . . ,' mused the Magistrate; and again,
  'Hum . . . ,'
And 'Bless my soul!' and 'Shame!' and 'Come, come,
  come!'

'Cats have their territory,' Davy said,
And blinked, and tried to think, and scratched his
  head.

and is warned

My good man,
you're a sad disgrace to the Human Race,
and that just about sums up this case!

The Law can
show no mercy to pig-headed fellows who
insist on never doing what they're told to do.

In your eyes,
you may well have been appearing, throughout this
    hearing,
as the victim of Traffic Engineering.

You'd be wise
to reflect that we're – let me make this clear –
only trying to help you, by bringing you here.

Now take heed!
Your house will come down, and you'll do as the
    Town
Clerk says, so don't go looking for a martyr's crown.

You are freed –
but never again dare to climb into that box when I'm
on this Bench, or as sure as Court bells chime,
                              I'll give you Time!

he inquires about Time

Daft Davy to himself: 'What's Time?' –
    Till the question pulsed in his brain.
Then he sought for replies from the clever and wise;
    But all his asking was vain.

The Policeman to Daft Davy: 'Why,
    Time's a dark cell and windows with bars;
Time's the oakum you pick when we put you in nick,
    With no sun and no moon and no stars.'

But how, O how, can Time see to run,
With no light from the stars, the moon and the sun?

The Vicar to Davy: 'My son,
    There's no Time in the World-Without-End.
That the Heavenly Flock should have need of a clock
    May God, in his goodness, forfend!'

Is God so poor, and His Blessèd Flock,
That between them they can't afford a gold clock?

The Philosopher to Daft Davy: 'Come,
    Time's merely a word – an illusion!
I most firmly insist that it doesn't exist,
    So let that put an end to confusion.'

That word can hurt more than sticks and stones,
For it's made your head bald and dried your bones!

Mad Blanche to her brother: 'Time runs
    As water runs by in the river:
We are all of us drops, and the flood never stops,
    For it's raining for ever and ever . . .'

Mad Blanche becomes a vagrant

With her mog and her dog and her home wrapped in
  black plastic bags
she sold matches at street-ends and bus stops, or
  rummaged stale bread
from foul trashheaps and dustbins, or begged
  outside pubs, or lay dead
to the world all night through in shop doorways –
  a huddle of rags.

They'd have swept her away with the garbage, or
  what's even worse,
they'd have put down her mog and her dog and then
  clamped her Inside;
but they feared her mad eyes, her wild hair, and
  drew back, terrified,
when she raved like a banshee, curdling their blood
  with her curse.

and Davy, likewise

He sat with his legs stiff as parallel bars
By the Newsagent's shop, at the pavement's end,
With his cloth cap upturned and empty as air
Save for fleas and the hope that his luck would mend.

They drew up in their pairs in white Panda cars
With: 'Hullo, then! What *have* we got here?'
With: 'Hoy, you! On yer feet!' and 'Just keep off our
    beat,
Or we'll slap you Inside. Is that clear?'

They kept moving him on from back lanes and back-
    alleys,
From benches in Station and Precinct and Square,
From Car Parks and Toilets and Churchyard
    tombstones
And doorways and cellars God only knows where.

He slept in the end in the rusting Bandstand
With his marmalade tom and a troubled brain –
How the weeping dark and derelict park
Could be Home was beyond his poor wits to explain!

he sneaks into the Cathedral

He kept to the back, away from the smells
And the bells.

Among the pillars the voices soared
To the Lord.

Robed in the pulpit the Bishop chanted
And ranted.

He said they should give and not be greedy
To the needy.

He said they should succour the poor
Who lived next door.

He said everyone's the brother
Of one another.

Davy stood, not daring to sit down,
All on his own.

Then out they all trooped, talking at ease,
Rattling car keys.

The Bishop passed him when it was over,
Driving his Rover.

The smell of the old Cathedral
Seemed lethal.

he walks in the night

Climbing rung after rung the scrambling-
    net of the skies,
Above roof-top and Quayside crane
    went Davy's eyes.

They glinted in primitive wonder
    with starlight thrown
At Daft Davy a thousand years
    before he was born.

And rung after painful rung, his slow
    thoughts climbed the night –
Cat-walking roof and chimney-pot
    at a dizzying height –
Till they slipped and were tumbled headlong
    into strange seas of light.

he dies

Daft Davy swore by his four wits
    He'd get the better of time;
He took a Woolworth's watch to bits
    And flung it into the Tyne.

That afternoon the sun went down,
    At night the moon uprose;
And Davy, since they wouldn't drown,
    Hid under the bedclothes.

He bandaged his eyes with rags and string,
    He plugged his ears with straw;
Day broke with never a bird to sing,
    Night came with never a star.

But still his pulse went tick-a-teg,
    And still his breath kept time;
He nipped his nose in an old clothes-peg
    And tied his wrists with the line.

Daft Davy lay doggo till he died
    A silent, stubborn death:
All under the blankets he defied
    The clock that beat in his breath.

and is buried

At the funeral of Daft Davy
    The coal-black drizzle wept
On Mad Blanche and the undertaker
    And the magpie priest who kept
Mumbling to himself, or perhaps to his Maker.

The hearse wasn't followed by adults
    Under the seeping skies,
But Mad Blanche caught a marmalade tom
    Out of her weeping eyes;
And a dirty, damp handful of lads, God knows where
    from.

And the magpie priest kept mumbling
    Of 'Davy our brother';
And the layabout lads couldn't stop
    From nudging each other
As the wet clay beat a tattoo on the coffin top;

For each of them knew that Daft Davy
    Was the twin of all
Who're shiftless, jobless, down on their luck . . .
    As they left the funeral
The tom-cat howled at the grave, like a creature
    struck.

Epitaph

Underneath this wormy earth
Lies Daft Davy who, at birth,
Joined for life (it so pleased God)
As Private in the Awkward Squad.

Feckless, lazy, couldn't-care-less,
Dolt and dunce, and one hell of a mess.
Gentle reader, do not laugh –
This is in part *your* Epitaph!